Robert Bird

More Law Lyrics

Robert Bird

More Law Lyrics

ISBN/EAN: 9783744769037

Printed in Europe, USA, Canada, Australia, Japan

Cover: Foto ©Andreas Hilbeck / pixelio.de

More available books at **www.hansebooks.com**

MORE LAW LYRICS

BY

ROBERT BIRD

AUTHOR OF 'LAW LYRICS,' ETC.

WILLIAM BLACKWOOD AND SONS
EDINBURGH AND LONDON
MDCCCXCVIII

CONTENTS.

———

CONTENTS.

And now let me draw,
  Like lovely red coral,
From oceans of law,
  This beautiful moral :—
If ever you be
Red hot for a plea,
Sit back and keep cool,
  Your judgment to titivate,
And then, as a rule,
  You'll see cause to mitigate
Your ardour for rackets,
And dusting of jackets,
And, if you've a doubt,
Be wise, and back out ;—
Spill barrels of ink, but don't litigate.

MORE LAW LYRICS.

———

YOU NEVER CAN TELL.

You never can tell till the case is decided,
   Which way the decision will go ;
The best fighting plea that was ever provided
   May melt like a handful of snow.
   With findings in fact, and findings in law,
   With precedents old, and distinctions to draw,
Oh ! you never can tell till the case is decided,
   Which way the decision will go.

To Counsel your hopes and your fears you've confided,
   His learned opinion to know,
Who shows you how hairs can be split and divided,
   And feathers turn scales to and fro.

A

For often the best and the simplest appeals
　　Have axles on axles, and wheels within wheels ;
Oh ! you never can tell till the case is decided,
　　Which way the decision will go.

Some Lords put their wigs on a trifle one-sided,
　　And some pull them down very low ;
And clients at times have believed they were guided
　　By watching these signals—although,
　　　Were all the full bench to sit nidding and nodding,
　　　While junior counsel are pleading and plodding ;
Oh ! you never can tell till the case is decided,
　　Which way the decision will go.

GOWF IS A GAME.

Oh ! Gowf is a game
    That we a' hae to learn ;
It may be as a patriarch,
    It may be as a bairn.
But, whether late or early,
    When ance we get the ca',
We're as keen as any caddy
    For a rattle at the ba'.

      A wee rappie o't, and a wee rappie o't;
      Oh, we're aye a deal the better for
      A wee rappie o't.

Some find their joy in curling-stanes,
    And some in rowin' balls,
And some upon the heather hills,
    And some in gilded halls ;
But on this earth there's nothing makes
    A healthy, happy Scot,
Like touching up the gutta wi'
    A wee rappie o't.

A LEGAL EPISODE.

YES, she was young and tall and fair,
  And in my dusky room
The lustre of her golden hair
  Shot sunshine through the gloom ;
Yes, she was rich, and would be wise
  With sips from wisdom's cup,
And as she sipped, her soft brown eyes
  Looked down, and sometimes up.

"Pray tell me, man of law," she said,
  "Why I have got a vote ?"
"Because of taxes, simple maid—
  Of that pray make a note."
She glanced demurely at her rings—
  "Then tell me, if you please,
Since I may vote for Boards and things,
  Why not for our M.P.'s ?"

Her question and her upward look,
   Her ribbons, frills, and laces,
Like Joshua's trump, most roughly shook
   My Jericho of cases.
With laughter lurking on her lip,
   Her bright eyes on me fixed,
I felt my logic losing grip,
   My statutes getting mixed.

I sought a book of hoary years,
   A relic of the Fall,
And read that women, idiots, peers,
   Are equal, equal all.
"Oh, really!" and she sweetly smiled,
   "You lawyers are strange folks;
Who could have guessed that you beguiled
   Your time with writing jokes!"

I told her next what statesmen say,
   That women have no right
To vote in an Imperial way,
   Because they cannot fight.
"Indeed! How chivalrous, how kind!
   And yet I understand
That all the lame and halt and blind
   Have votes throughout the land."

I must have paused and faltered then,
   For she addressed me thus : ·
" I cannot comprehend why men
   Are so absurd with us.
They say our muscle, nerve, and brain
   Are feeble, weak, and green—
I wonder, and you might explain,
   How England has a Queen?

" I've read in speeches full of grace !
   That, led like geese along,
We'd vote for every pretty face,
   And everything that's wrong."
" Oh ! " I exclaimed, " these are the things
   Which men say when they're stumping,
Full of spontaneous wit, that springs
   Like water raised with pumping !

" Each cock-eared ass must have his bray,
   His windy lungs to clear—
There's nothing cheaper in our day
   Than eloquence, my dear !
The pot may call the kettle black,
   But that is hardly proof
That every kettle has a crack
   Or else a cloven hoof ! "

She rose and thanked me much for that
  Which I had made so plain,
And as she tricked her veil and hat,
  Inquired if it would rain,
Remarking, " You must not be too
  Hooked in with legal hooks,
For I'm a Girton Girl, and you
  Are.better than your books."

I bowed her gently to the door,
  And out into the air,
And as I crossed my office floor
  And sank into my chair,
Now that the interview was done,
  The question seemed to be,
Which had advised the other one,
  And which way lay the fee ?

A WIGLESS BENCH.

THE mighty Lord Chief Justice Russell
   In court, with windows open wide,
Sat with slow-melting brain and muscle,
   Iced water twinkling by his side ;
Ermine and lace embowered the Ruler,
   A yard-long wig embraced his head,
But still, instead of getting cooler,
   His face assumed a fiercer red.

Queen's Counsel, moist as glossy leeches,
   Were dripping at the chin and nose—
The only dry thing was their speeches—
   When suddenly his Lordship rose.
"Oh ! this is really too oppressive ! "—
   'Twas not their speeches, but the heat.
Off flew his gown—still more aggressive,
   He banged his wig upon his seat !

Electrified by his example,
    Cottons and silks forgot their pride ;
Wigs, ties, and gowns, both scant and ample,
    Were tossed about on every side !
The roof fell not, although the ceiling
    Had never felt so great a wrench,
As gownless Barristers appealing
    For justice to a wigless Bench !

Across the blue Atlantic Ocean
    There is a hot and happy land,
Where Judges sit and hear a motion
    In shirt-sleeves, with a pipe in hand ;
And while that might be hardly fitting,
    What could be nicer—what think you ?—
Than gentlemen of Justice sitting
    In brindled locks and black surtout ?

SCOTLAND'S CREESHY POUNDS.

The spendthrift says the guinea's round,
   That it may run in rings;
The miser sings that he has found
   It flat, to lie in bings.
Whate'er may be the guinea's use,
   Odds! gramercie and zounds!
There's not a shade of an excuse
   For Scotland's creeshy pounds.

One day a hungry poet wrote,
   In language brisk and terse,
Upon an English five-pound note
   A rare immortal verse;
Of how it slowly came in sight,
   And sped away in bounds;
That verse to-day he could not write
   On Scotland's creeshy pounds.

Were he to try his furious pen,
   He might, with blabs and blots,
Write, like some oily-footed hen,
   In kicks, and scarts, and dots—
" The love of gold gets mickle blame
   Where little fault abounds,
But filthy lucre is the name
   For Scotland's creeshy pounds."

The country's overdone with banks,
   In buildings rich and fine,
That pay out dividends of thanks,
   As from a diamond-mine;
But it would some folk better please,
   On sanitary grounds,
Were they to make an annual bleeze
   Of Scotland's creeshy pounds.

NATURE'S CALENDAR.

THE bird that sang so sweetly on the spray,
And with loud music roused the sleeping day,
Hailing the dawn ere yet had fled the dark—
Was it the blackbird, robin, linnet, lark?
Nay! 'twas the thrush who, with his challenge mellow,
Awoke the world with calling to his fellow
To mark the east, where, in faint rosy dyes,
The door of heaven was opening down the skies
With bars of gold, and crimson curtains drawn,
To kindle on the hills the fires of dawn.

The flower that burned so brightly on the ground,
And with her beauty sweetened all around,
Worshipping lowly where the river flows—
Was it the pansy, tulip, lily, rose?
Nay! 'twas the little Celandine of gold,
Whose face to clouds of red she did uphold,

Watching, until her lover in the sky,
The glittering sun, should catch her glistening eye,
And with one dewdrop, for a mirror given,
Renew sweet correspondence with her heav'n.

Let Almanacs declare that Winter's here,
Sweet flowers do better Calendar the year ;
The songs of birds tell more of times and seasons
Than all the ologists with all their reasons.
Ere the Snow-king has with his darts retreated,
The cheerful sparrow tells him he's defeated,
And little hands of snowdrop, primrose, crocus,
Bid him take off his blustering hocus-pocus ;
And soon the world, reconquered from the cold,
Rolls a green ball with daffodils of gold.

And so would I, in pages thin and narrow,
Repeat the chirrup of the sprightly sparrow—
Bid all my readers shake the ice and snow
From their dull wits, and let blithe humour flow ;
For in this little volume you will find
A merry book best suits a merry mind.

POOR COLIN'S GOWN.

Poor Colin's gown is very brown,
    And when you come to look through it,
It hangs so frail about the tail,
    An owl could read a book through it.

For Colin's court of chief resort
    Is where the fires so blazingly
Warm up the flanks of hams and shanks,
    Enjoying life amazingly.

His horse-hair wig of fur and rig
    Has smaller grown with shrinking o't;
A legal drum it has become
    With thumping law, and thinking o't.

In carving joints of legal points
    His tongue has much of wit in it,
For, while you stare, he'll split a hair,
    And find two more to split in it.

The only Lord whose mighty word
    Can quite fulfil his prophecies,
Is one whose nod can show the road
    To all the public offices.

And so he sings with tattered wings—
    " Hay! cherry chum! cum derry dum!
Come sure, come slow, some day I'll crow,
    A cock within a Sherra-dum! "

THE CURLING-STONE.

THERE's music in the curling-stone,
   There's singing on the rink !
And sweeter echoes know I none
   Than stones that meet and clink.
With white ice glistening on the slide,
   And snow on bank and brae,
On golden feet the minutes glide,
   And too short seems the day !

The skip has held his broom on high,
   And he has laid it down ;
A leading stone, is still his cry,
   Upon the pot-lid's crown.
"It comes ! it comes ! up cowes !" they shout,
   As it goes gliding by,
But soon a rival knocks him out
   With gentle chap and lie.

Forefinger out, wee finger in,
   Come up the crowding stones,
And still they soop them as they spin,
   With many sighs and groans.
Oh, for a guard of solid rock !
   But still they pack the head,
Till, dashing, crashing comes the shock,
   That clears the ring instead.

The huntsman loves the bounding steed,
   The fisher, foaming falls—
The sportsman makes lead bullets speed,
   The golfer, gutty balls ;
But curling takes a blacksmith's hand,
   Bairn's touch, and falcon's eye,
A bullet up the slide to land,
   Or cuddle in and lie !

THE LAWYER'S CAT.

LET the truth at once be written
  Now, I sing about a cat
That has never been a kitten,
  That has never smelt a rat;
But of tails she has as many
  As a tinker's tab has lives,
Tails that wag as fast as any
  Tongues of wives, wives, wives!

Once the cats—the gay deceivers—
  Down in Egypt, we are told,
Were much worshipped by believers,
  Sitting upon thrones of gold;
And I'm certain no one grudges
  That our whisking little wench
Should sit down with British Judges
  On the bench, bench, bench!

For we're troubled—greatly troubled—
  With the brute who kicks his wife,
With the wretch with fist up-doubled,
  With the fiend who draws his knife ;
And while some think prison raiment
  Is enough to purge the sin,
Others say they need repayment
  On their skin, skin, skin !

But we're told that bareback thrashing
  Tends to brutalise the breast ;
That for stabbing, kicking, gashing,
  Gentle treatment is the best.
But for men who maim and ravish,
  With no soul above a rat,
The best beast to tame the savage
  Is the cat, cat, cat !

THE MAVIS SINGS.

The hyacinth rings, on bells of blue,
The hours of spring, the green wood through;
With speckled throat and dusky wings
The mavis sings! the mavis sings!
Go, find a maid, and love her well,
And she may love *thee*—who can tell?

A crimson blush on clouds of rose
As quickly comes, as quickly goes;
The smiles of April's golden sun
To shadows run! to shadows run!
She loves thee now, but, maids are strange,
And, though thou kiss her, she may change.

The hawthorn by the spreading oak
Hath donned her fragrant bridal cloak;

And if she will not wed to-day,
Some day she may ! some day she may !
Tell her the love grows never cold
That sits within a ring of gold.

And if to-day she will not wed,
Shake down the blossoms on her head,
And say, again upon the tree
They ne'er can be ! they ne'er can be !
And all the kisses kissed below
She shall not have them back—oh no !

BROTHER JONATHAN'S ROCKET.

He crammed it with lightning and thunder,
  John Bull with its roar to affright,
And make him feel humble, and wonder
  If all the wide heavens were alight,
      And bow his lone head
      To stripes that are red,
  And forty-nine stars blue and white.

John heard the loud swish of the rocket,
  And, though it seemed aimed at his eye,
His heart did not sink in its socket,
  Or jump at the signs in the sky;
      For, somehow or other,
      He guessed that his brother
  Was trying a bit of high-fly.

It seemed that Miss Venezuela,
 In regions of rock, swamp, and furze,
Was spreading her crimson umbrella
 O'er portions of plateaus and spurs
  Where John, *primo loco*,
  Beyond Orinoco,
Had rights that were older than hers.

With nudges and nips, all quite legal,
 These two were intent on their game,
When Jonathan straddled his eagle,
 And set all the furze in a flame,
  By saying he'd draw
  A line with his claw,
And make John Bull keep to the same.

Come! Jonathan, come! you're in danger
 Of mixing up "must do" with "might,"
For, how would you like if some stranger,
 Some fine shiny morning, should write,
  That in a few weeks
  You'd got to eat leeks,
And munch them in silence, or fight?

No! Jonathan, no! when you're cooler,
 You'll grant that, with hints from your boot,

To ask John to smell the thick ruler
  Would hardly conclude the dispute ;
    Let others shoot others,
    The friendship of brothers
  Is dearer than swamp, the square foot.

And yet, if his title be shady,
  It hardly becomes an old knight
To shun a quadrille with a lady
  Who scarce knows her left from her right ;
    Assured the true bend
    Will show in the end,
  When everything's brought to the light.

THE LAWYER'S WOOING.

THERE was a lawyer and a lass—
  Pursuer and defender;
There was a lawyer and a lass,
And though his brow was bold as brass,
  The maid would not surrender.
'Twas thus his woful case he pled—
  " You cannot slight or pass it;"
'Twas thus his woful case he pled—
" For somehow I have somewhere read,
  Lex nihil frustra facit.

If condescendence do but meet
  With answers soft replying;
If condescendence do but meet,
Love is a process soon complete,
  And ready for the tying.

What though I've written prose and rhyme,
  And oft with them attacked you ;
What though I've written prose and rhyme,
Let's jettison my load of crime,
  Lex Rhodia de jactu.

" I'll never more say black is white,
  Or even kind of greyish ;
I'll never more say black is white,
And ever in the hardest fight
  Be gayest of the gayish.
Thus daily will my love be shown,
  Probatio probata ;
Thus daily will my love be shown,
I long to call you all my own,
  Invecta et illata !

" When autumn turns me out of courts,
  In green sequestered places ;
When autumn turns me out of courts,
I'll read you curious law reports
  Of matrimonial cases.
And there we'll woo the Muses, O !
  Soon may you know what that is ;
And there we'll woo the Muses, O !
Cum decimis inclusis, O !
  Et nunquam separatis.

" A ring of gold without alloy
   Is Cupid's charming fetter;
A ring of gold without alloy,
And all through life 'twill be a joy—
   No diamonds could be better.
'Twill kindle courage, banish fear,
   And every trouble cure, O !
'Twill kindle courage, banish fear,
And mark you sweetly as my dear
   Sponsalia de futuro.

" Weigh well my pleas in love and law,
   Abandon your defences;
Weigh well my pleas in love and law,
A sweet joint-minute let us draw,
   Dividing our expenses.
We'll say not who's been best advised,
   Nor who the strongest hand is;
We'll say not who's been best advised,
But that the suit's been compromised
   Mutatis et mutandis."

The maiden sighed with heart aflame
   Beneath her lace and satin;
The maiden sighed with heart aflame
Each time she heard the youth declaim
   His mingled love and Latin.

And answered in her own sweet way,
　　Unskilled in Latin's uses;
And answered in her own sweet way—
"I do so like to hear you say—
　　Cum decimis inclusis!"

A REPLY.*

"Beware! Beware!" the maiden said,
    "I know those Latin phrases;
Beware! Beware!" the maiden said,
"For I've been taught that language dead—
    Its numbers, genders, cases.
Once on a time 'twas not the rule,
    I do confess, *instanter;*
Once on a time 'twas not the rule
To teach these things to maids at school,
    Sed tempora mutantur.

"And when those ancient words you use,
    They're not beyond my knowledge;
And when those ancient words you use,
They're not to me the least abstruse,
    Because I've been to college.

* By permission of the author, Mr Archibald Campbell.

I've read Horatian, Livian lore,
  Of Chloë, and of Phyllis;
I've read Horatian, Livian lore,
For, *tempora mutantur*—more
  Et nos mutamur illis.

" I'm skilled in mathematics, too,
  In calculus and equation;
I'm skilled in mathematics, too,
Because you know I have been through
  The higher education.
And when you offer me your hand
  And *cardiac-organum ;*
And when you offer me your hand,
I'd like to clearly understand
  How much you have *per annum.*

" For if we were engaged, you see,
  I've such a cultured sense;
For if we were engaged, you see,
To make appropriate gifts to me
  Would cost you some expense.
And ere we reached the final point
  Of *virum et uxorem ;*
And ere we reached the final point,
I'd have to estimate the joint
  Communio bonorum.

" You say a ring without alloy
　　Will care and trouble banish ;
You say a ring without alloy
Will make our lives a time of joy,
　　Whence every fear will vanish.
How nice of you ! romantic quite
　　A sentiment like that is ;
How nice of you ! romantic quite,
Although it sounds a little trite,
　　Res meræ facultatis.

" You'll read me legal cases !　There,
　　That's not so nice as rings ;
You'll read me legal cases !　There,
I'd rather go to places where
　　They've men, and fun, and things.
I'd like a little flirting, too,
　　Though quite devoid of malice ;
I'd like a little flirting, too,
Before I say I'll give to you
　　Potestas maritalis.

"I don't dislike you, not a bit !
　　Yes, you may call again ;
I don't dislike you, not a bit,
You really seem a trifle hit—
　　It's just the way with men.

But if you come, you understand
  Periculo petenti ;
But if you come, you understand
I'm not prepared to give my hand
  Ad primo venienti.

THE LAWS OF ANCIENT GOLF.

When James the Second was our king,
  It did his feelings harrow,
That men would rather drive the ball
  Than shoot the whizzing arrow;
And since they played the game of Golf
  On every day but one day,
He bade them bring their bows to church,
  And shoot their shots on Sunday.

At every Parish Kirk, he said,
  Two butts should be erected,
At which each man could shoot six shots,
  And have his bow inspected;
And all who failed six shots to shoot—
  Herds, blacksmiths, souters, bakers—
Must pay a fine of fourpence Scots,
  For drink for the bowmakers.

c

When James the Third came to the throne,
   He ordered all his bowmen
Who could not hit these ample butts
   To arm themselves as yeomen,
And do with axe and hairy targe
   The goose-step on the heather;
Remarking, that their arms would cost
   Scarce one good hide of leather.

The wily game of Golf, he said,
   Had got so firm a footing,
It must be "putten doun," or men
   Would lose all skill in shooting.
And that it was his royal will
   In this important matter,
All men should learn with bow and shaft
   The English ranks to scatter.

When James the Fourth put on the crown,
   He stamped his foot down, saying,
He soon would pass a sharp-set law
   To end this false golf-playing;
And then, with drum and touting-horn,
   On open grass or hidden,
All such unprofitable sports
   As golfing were forbidden.

That all the people might observe
    Their royal master's orders,
Each peaceful parish green must have
    Two butts within its borders;
And that a forty-shilling fine
    Would lie where'er 'twas "funden,"
That shooting was not practised there
    As it by law was "bunden."

Illegal then were cleek and club,
    Unlawful, drives and teeing;
Forbidden was the shortest putt
    Of any human being!
The peaceful lovers of the game
    Had not the lives of sparrows,
And all that English ribs might feel
    The sting of Scottish arrows.

Now merry Arthur is the king,
    And core of golfing laddies,
And he, at Chiselhurst, has said,
    Before the English caddies,
Four hundred years have amply proved,
    With hazards, holes, and bunkers,
'Tis not the arrow, but the ball,
    The Englishman that conquers!

OUR PAUPERS.

There's a refuge for the aged,
　　And a haven for the poor,
Where their bed and bread are certain,
　　And their clothing is made sure,—
With a visit from the Doctor
　　When the body needs repair,
And a sermon from the Chaplain
　　On the mansions in the air.

It is called The People's Poorhouse,
　　Kept up by the people's rates,
But the people hate this haven
　　With the bitterest of hates ;
And the best among the poorest
　　To their graves would rather go,
Than approach the dreaded portals
　　Of this very House of Woe !

There are pensions for the wealthy,
　　There are pensions for the great,
And the man who gets a pension
　　Gets it on a silver plate;
But the worn-out toiler's pittance,
　　Which the hoary head should crown,
Is bestowed by grudging fingers
　　With a kick and cuff and frown.

And yet, many people wonder,
　　And they cannot understand—
Why this People's Institution
　　Is detested in the land.
Wisdom says there is a reason
　　For all things beneath the sun,
And, an inch below the surface,
　　There is often more than one.

There the criminal and honest,
　　There the profligate and pure,
Have to meet and mix together
　　On the common ground of "poor."
There the bonds are torn asunder
　　That have lasted all the life—
Children from the weeping mother,
　　Husband from the aged wife.

For we're told that being beggars
  Is so pleasant to the mind,
That our charity must ever
  Be with punishment combined ;
So the Guardians of the Parish
  Need to guard with iron hand,
Lest the voice of singing paupers
  Should be heard within the land.

Is old age so full of honey
  That it needs some drops of gall ?
Is misfortune so delightful
  That we should increase the fall ?
And is wealth so universal
  In this very golden time,
That we must, in common fairness,
  Look on poverty as crime ?

Oh ! we hear so much of pensions
  Now, to help the feeble poor,
And of all the good intentions
  Now, to make old age secure ;
It were worth our while to ponder,
  If the kernel in the shell
Be not, how to make the Poorhouse
  More a home and less a hell.

WINDY GOLD.

THERE are clove pinks in my garden,
　　Crimson roses on the wall,
But the face that's at the window
　　Is the sweetest of them all ;
With her hair of primrose yellow,
　　And her cheeks of peachy hue,
And a hundred childish fancies
　　In her little head of two.

You can trip her with your slipper,
　　You can take her with your toe,
And she screams and nips and dances,
　　Till you laugh and let her go.
On your knee, if you would keep her—
　　Oh, she is a naughty chit !—
She will bribe you for her freedom
　　With a kiss, and then a hit.

She makes raids on silver daisies,
　　And bright buttercups of brass,
Till her snowy little apron
　　Is a sack of flowers and grass ;
And she loves to take the pansies,
　　All asleep in fragrant beds,
And to fill her pink sun-bonnet
　　With their little purple heads.

There are diamonds in her glances,
　　There are pearls between her lips,
With her laughter and her prattle,
　　And her kisses and her nips.
Not for all the shining treasure
　　Which the rocks of crystal hold,
Would I give my small pea-blossom
　　With her locks of windy gold !

YOUR HAND, UNCLE SAM!

Your hand, Uncle Sam!
   'Tis true, we've had words,
But slit be the tongue
   That first talks of swords.
Let's draw up a bond
   'Tween nation and nation,
To square all disputes
   By fair arbitration.

In Court we can kick
   And cuff and call names,
Then rap for the bill
   And settle our claims;
As good as a war
   For letting off vapour,
With bullets of ink
   And targets of paper.

We're sprigs of one tree,
  Of thorns and of roses,
By proof of blue eyes,
  Red cheeks, and sharp noses :
Our girls with their hair
  So raven and flaxen ;
Our boys with their tongues
  So honest and Saxon.

There's grit in us both,
  Enough for true brothers,
To take sauce from each,
  But sauce from no others.
Oh yes ! we once tried
  Our strength in a manner—
Then Johnny got kicks,
  And Sam a starred banner.

Face round and grip hands,
  And grip with such heart
That no power on earth
  Shall wrench us apart ;
And so let us teach
  Our children at school—
To give while they can
  Christ's kingdom a pull.

BY YON BURNSIDE.

Oн! gin I were by yon burnside
   Where linties sing sae cheerie, O !
I'd turn my face to Minnie's cot,
   And whistle for my dearie, O !
And be she in, or be she out,
   I warrant she will hear me, O !
Oh ! gin I were by yon burnside
   Where linties sing sae cheerie, O !

Down where the hazels kiss the stream
   Young love did first bewitch her, O !
As, blushing, on the stepping-stone
   She let me dip her pitcher, O !
And ilka time she comes that road
   She gangs awa' the richer, O !
Down where the hazels kiss the stream
   Young love did first bewitch her, O !

Were I behind yon elder-bush,
  And Minnie close beside me, O !
I'd place a red rose in her breast,
  And speir gin she could bide me, O !
I'd fauld her in my loving arms
  Wi' trembling leaves to hide me, O !
Were I behind yon elder-bush,
  And Minnie close beside me, O !

A MILLION, OR MORE.

THERE once was a nation called Sparta,
  Whose law was the word of their King,
And though they had no Magna Charta,
  The people could laugh, dance, and sing.
But let not the notion disturb us,
  Though fierce and despotic his rule,
The laws that were made by Lycurgus
    Might send us to school.

He saw, that like bees upon honey,
  The race after wealth was so hot
That men thought too much about money,
  Too little of how it was got;
And just as a sort of environ,
  To limit this folly, we're told,
He ordered a coinage of iron,
    And banished the gold.

And so, when a thief dreamt of stealing,
    Or judges of bribes had a thought,
The trouble that lay in concealing
    Was more than the prize that it brought;
While men with a turn to play miser
    Found cartloads of iron a bore,
And people inclined to be wiser
    Sought money no more.

Now, how would it do if 'twere written
    Of all with a million or more,
Who slave-drive the toilers in Britain
    And heap up their treasures in store,
Each year, as their bank account waxes,
    The law a fat slice should secure,
To keep down the national taxes
    And help up the poor?

THE VICTORY OF WORDS.

'Tis very nice to walk about
   With golfers on the green,
Where cowslips grow, and talk about
   The early pea and bean ;
But have you ever thought about
   The devilry of swords,
And how the law has brought about
   The victory of words ?

It used to be the fashion once,
   When men had legal rights,
To prove them in a passion once
   With broken heads in fights ;
But prince and peer and peasant now
   Fight out their fights at law,
And ruddy gold, so pleasant now,
   Is all the blood they draw.

Since broken bones in duel have
    Gone fairly out of season,
And Courts, with paper fuel, have
    Brought in the reign of reason ;
Since right can be relied upon,
    'Tween man and brother man,
It surely might be tried upon
    A more extended plan.

But then we're told a curious thing,
    More fitting long-eared asses,
That fair-play is a spurious thing
    Applied to men in masses ;
That justice, pressed upon her, is
    What every nation shuns,
And that a kingdom's honour is
    A thing for swords and guns.

And when two nations quarrel, they
    Hang up the scales at once,
And grasping the gun-barrel, they
    Cry, Justice is a dunce !
That right and wrong and kindness are
    For cockerels and pullets,
And people steeped in blindness are,
    Who favours brains, not bullets.

And statesmen keep declaring to
   The sun, and moon, and stars,
They only are preparing to
   Avert all kinds of wars;
That peaceful arbitration is
   In abstract very good,
But arming all the nation
   Is the way to cool the blood.

And just by way of showing that
   They never mean to fight,
Our armies are so growing that
   No man can count their might;
All massing and all moving, just
   Like clouds that still increase,
Intent on one day proving just
   That lightning makes for peace.

I hear the anvils sounding in
   The march of coming years,
Where law is slowly pounding in
   To pruning-hooks men's spears.
Strike hard, ye lawyer fellows! for
   The forge is roaring wide,
And kings may blow the bellows, for
   You've God upon your side!

D

WHEN COWSLIPS SHINE.

Sing me a song of early Spring,
    When blossom clouds the thorn,
And skylarks, high on fluttering wing,
    Bring in the rosy morn;
Then lambkins frisk upon the green,
    And cowslips shine with dew,
And every lover woos his lass
    That has a lass to woo.

Who would not be a shepherd-boy
    To win a sunburnt maid,
With tales of love, of hope, of joy,
    Beneath the hawthorn's shade?
She is her father's pet, I ween,
    To keep her still he vows;
But love steals many an hour at e'en
    When milkmaids call their cows.

The speckled mavis in the tree
   May whistle loud and clear,
For he has got no eyes to see,
   And she no ears to hear;
The moments fly on wings of bliss—
   True love was ever so—
And still they have another kiss
   Before they part and go.

THE TAXATION.

OH, tax me not hard !
    Cried jolly Tom Sutty ;
He knew that his fees
    Were heavy as putty.
For little thought he,
    When things were less solemn,
That an Auditor's snuff
    Would sprinkle his column.

The old soldier smiled
    As his chair he adjusted,
And lifted his pen
    With blood of fees crusted.
" You cannot get this,
    And you cannot get that,"
With strokes right and left,
    Like the claws of a cat.

He cut to one-half
    Each five-shilling letter,
With sheets, pages, hours,
    The luck was no better;
And as the account
    Went down through the riddle,
A face like the moon
    Grew long as a fiddle.

And so for an hour,
    'Tween inking and drying,
Fast, heels over head,
    The charges went flying.
The Auditor laughed,
    And bent himself double,
When adding a fee
    To cover his trouble.

Roulette is a game
    With green cloth and border,
Where thieves are well paid
    To keep rogues in order;
The Lawyers, poor lads!—
    The joke's worth repeating—
Pay one of themselves
    To keep them from cheating!

Should tradesmen's accounts
  Turn out to be salted,
The seller's abased,
  The buyer exalted ;
But law is so strange,
  When taxing is ended,
The client's ashamed,
  The Lawyer offended.

SURPLUS LAND.

THE fishers launched their shining smack,
    And filled it full of heather,
And sailed the Duchess out and back,
    Her and the Duke together;
But not a sixpence would they take,
    Unblushing and undaunted,
Until his Grace said, he would make
    Them tell what most they wanted.

Each fisher loved a bonnie lass
    With heart as hot as arson,
And all for lack of house and grass
    They could not fee the parson;
And so they said, a bit of land
    Would suit them beyond measure;
The Duke replied, " See, there's my hand,
    I grant your wish with pleasure."

And scarce six months had come and gone,
    And long they lagged and tarried,
Till Archie, Katie, Bell, and John,
    Were snugly housed and married ;
The envy of the neighbour-folk,
    Who all for land were wishing,
But 'tis not every day Dukes joke,
    Or Duchesses go fishing.

Our Parliament may all command,
    And strong hands can compel it,
And when a Railway wishes land,
    The titled laird must sell it ;
And if he names a ransom price,
    And on his acres sticks it,
Two arbiters, as meek as mice,
    Step in between and fix it.

We're told that Railways got this vote
    To benefit the nation,
And that's just why we should promote
    Our cottar population ;
For why should squires hold up the land,
    And Parliament allow it,
When honest men with gold in hand
    Are begging leave to plough it ?

THROUGH CHECKERED WOODS.

THROUGH checkered woods, upon a summer's day,
From homes of men I picked my easy way,
To meditate upon this life's small part,
And lay the balm of silence to my heart;
Armed with a little six-stopped pipe of wood,
To fill with music should it suit my mood,
And blow soft solace through the leafy covers—
Sweet stay of all philosophers and lovers.

Engaged with quiet thoughts, in pleased content
Along the clovered grassy glades I went,
With here a bosky thorn in snowy bloom,
And there a hyacinth bed of blue perfume,
While knotted branches twistingly outspread
A sun-shot roof of green above my head;

Till, coming to a stout oak reaching wide,
I leant my shoulder to his mossy side ;
And while my doggie, tired with many a chase,
Sat down with much contentment in his face,
I drew my pipe, and blew a prelude brief
To chorus sounds of breeze and tickling leaf :—
A few mixed notes of gratitude and hope
For all the tasks with which I had to cope ;
Then, having fingered out my little strain,
I stuck my pipe into my belt again.

Few thoughts had come and gone, till one by one
A choir of feathered songsters hymned the sun :
The mavis, merle, and redbreast's triple song
Most sweetly led the warbling airs along ;
And list'ning there, I heard in one brief minute,
The chaffinch, bulfinch, wren, and rosy linnet
With others join, and loudest did remark
The soaring raptures of the heavenly lark ;
And all this banquet, from true hearts outshaken,
Did one poor prelude on my pipe awaken.

Now, I in verse have preluded my song,
Which piping minds may merrily prolong ;
And as in woods no discord strikes the ear,
So in my notes no harshness you will hear,

But gentle satire when the magpie mocks,
And tickling fun when cuckoo double-knocks.
Kind reader, truth is humour's noblest leaven;
And should some line steal shafts of wit from heaven,
And should one thought your cloud of gloom disperse,
Then hail and keep a friend in that small verse.

THE PETTYFOGGER.

An auburn wig, and a wrinkled broo,
  He's a curious body a'thegither ;
At clippin' a lamb, or shearin' a soo—
  Gie him a hair, and he'll spin a tether.

He gies his advice in conundrums o' words,
  That, just as you want, turn ae road or ither ;
He'll crack by the hour upon widows' thirds—
  Gie him a hair, and he'll spin a tether.

At drawing a paper he's langsome and deep,
  At guiding a plea he's a vera bell-wether ;
Ower hillock and hollock he leads his sheep—
  Gie him a hair, and he'll spin a tether.

When fees fa' short, he's a corkit vial
  O' law, lear', and lees in a hide o' leather ;
A drum o' the best for a jury trial—
  Gie him a hair, and he'll spin a tether.

Fee him again, and you'll find him a vera
   Terrible dog to scent game in the heather ;
He scorns the decrees o' a Justice or Shirra—
   Gie him a hair, and he'll spin a tether.

He'll tell you the law's fu' o' whirligigs,
   And mark an appeal frae ae Court to anither,
And kittle up counsel and redd their wigs—
   Gie him a hair, and he'll spin a tether.

The Table o' Fees is his table o' fac's,
   At charging accounts he's a clerk o' the weather ;
Tak' tent o' his letters and couthie cracks—
   Gie him a hair, and he'll spin a tether.

THISTLEDOWN.

SWEET Thistledown! your hair's soft hue
   Is paler than the primrose sweet;
Your eyes are pansies, faintly blue;
   Your lips are where carnations meet.
What though your arms just bend and beat
   A yard above the daisy's head?
The journeys of your little feet
   Would tire a giant's foot to tread.

When first into my heart you crept,
   You found another sitting there—
A winsome maid that I have kept
   For-ever young, for-ever fair,
With just such eyes, and just such hair
   As yours, sweet puff of Thistledown!
But with this difference, I declare—
   She wears a dear, old-fashioned gown.

To some rare heart, ere youth be spent,
   One day your being will incline ;
And may you bring as sweet content
   As brought your mother's heart to mine.
Though mistress of a dearer shrine,
   If you be his and he be yours,
You'll none the less be ever mine,
   Sweet Thistledown ! while life endures.

TODDLIN' YET.

Wı' rosy cheeks and yellow hair!
   Toddlin' yet! and toddlin' yet!
A twalmonth old, and hardly mair,
Frae hand to hand, frae chair to chair,
He stumps, and stachers round the flair,
     Toddlin', toddlin' yet!

On daddie's stick he fain wad ride,
   Toddlin' yet, and toddlin' yet!
Wi' twa bricht een, sae blue and wide,
He dances at my armchair-side,
And oh! he is his mammie's pride,
     Toddlin', toddlin' yet!

He's just like monie other boys—
   Toddlin' yet, and toddlin' yet!

A vera rogue at makin' noise,
An unca scamp at breakin' toys,
Wi' little griefs, and mickle joys,
    Toddlin,' toddlin' yet!

Some day into the world he'll gang,
    Toddlin' yet, and toddlin' yet!
And there he'll meet wi' monie a bang;
May kind heav'n guide his feet alang,
To a' that's right—frae a' that's wrang,
    Toddlin', toddlin' yet!

THE LAW MILL.

If ever you snort
  And stamp for a case,
You'll find the Law Court
  A sort of mill-race,
That runs down a hill
To turn a strange mill,
That works with a laugh,
  And grinds with a squeal,
Where clients get chaff,
  And lawyers get meal;
The purpose to settle,
Who pot, and who kettle,
Which lively teetotum
Shall go to the bottom,
Which over, which under the wheel.

Some call it a dance
   Of red and white faces,
Where clients advance
   With grins and grimaces,
And lawyers in wigs
Arrange all the jigs,
And play diddle-diddle
   With skill and with ease,
Upon the bass-fiddle,
   For charges and fees ;
With witnesses swearing,
Affirming, declaring,
While calmly the Judge
Weighs fact against fudge,
Suspending his scales by the middle.

And now let me draw,
   Like lovely red coral,
From oceans of law,
   This beautiful moral :—
If ever you be
Red-hot for a plea,
Sit back and keep cool,
   Your judgment to titivate,
And then, as a rule,
   You'll see cause to mitigate

Your ardour for rackets,
And dusting of jackets,
And, if you've a doubt,
Be wise, and back out ;—
Spill barrels of ink, but don't litigate.

IN SUMMER'S NOON.

In Summer's noon, upon a rocky height
I rest awhile, to meditate and write.
'Mong stones and heather, round their bleating dams
In pairs and trios, frisk the woolly lambs,
While breaking waters, rushing, gushing near,
With sough of tree-tops, mingle in mine ear,—
Indeed, a scene more pastoral and sylvan
I could not wish beneath the blue pavilion.
   Below, a vale is sunnily outspread
From sparkling sea to far cloud-hooded head,
With here a knoll, and there a ridgy line,
Green marshalled with the lances of the pine ;
And where the crowding hazels droop and turn
Gold gravels flash, and paint the winding burn,
While rock and cliff lead up the pleasing view
From ruddy heath to mist-invading blue,

Where the hoar wardens of the valley rise,
And bathe their helms of silver in the skies.
Seen from a height like this, o'er earth's vast glen
How little are the strides of mighty men!
And measured by the calmness of these hills,
How fleeting are our joys, how brief our ills!

    Above, poured down from heav'n's high boundary wall,
Rains, hails, and snows, the mountain waterfall.
Forth launching from a cloven rocky pass,
It hangs in view, ere like a wave of glass
It glides clear down the moss-green slide, and shines,
As round rock-fronts and boulder-stones it twines;
From pool to granite pool of amber brown
It overflows, and breaking, tumbling down,
Cuts out of sight a channel in the cleft,
Till, angle caught, it shoots a dripping weft
Of crystal-threaded beads, with which it weaves
A sunny scarf, that signals through the leaves
Its downward leap, to where the naked rock,
Smoothed by the constant rub, with solid shock
Receives the wavering sheet of driving rain,
And makes the fount of diamonds leap again.

    There's laughter in that foam! there must be jokes
Among these stones round which the current pokes,
And through these granite basins, and like holes,
A stream of gentle humour surely rolls;

And why should not the toilers of the earth
Mix wit with work, and labour with like mirth?
Laugh, leap, and sparkle through the little space
That marks the limit of a mortal's race,—
Dropt from above, again we climb the skies;
In clouds we come, in clouds again we rise.

THE MEAL-MILLER.

THE Miller stands at his mill door,
   Contented aye, and dusty, O !
And keckles as he dings the stour
   Out frae his bonnet fusty, O !
Sae round a cheek, sae bricht an e'e,
   Wad mak' an auld stump flowery, O !
But Bessie says he daurna pree
   Her mou', wi' beard sae stoury, O !

The mill rins on frae early day,
   Wi' muckle din and clatter, O !
And better gear ye couldna hae
   Than wheels that row wi' water, O !
The birlin' stanes, the jinks, the shocks,
   Are music to the Miller, O !
For aye the meal that swalls his pocks
   His pouches fill wi' siller, O !

Some folk mak' broth o' nettles hot,
   And some mak' jell' o' rowans, O !
The dustings o' a Miller's coat
   Wad mak' a dish o' sowans, O !
And Bessie thinks so lane a life
   Some joy and pleasure misses, O !
And gin she were the Miller's wife
   She'd thole his dusty kisses, O !

OFF THE CHAIN.

Hurrah! for the glen with the heather!
  Glen Mavis, Glen Dove, and Glen Dhu!
Where sunshine and breezes together
  Have swept up the mist and the view.
A sigh for the Lord of Vacation,
  Waist-deep amid Motions and Bills,
While we, the true Lords of creation,
  Are drinking the nectar of hills!

Hurrah! for the Ben with the boulder,
  Ben Nevis, Ben Lomond, Ben A'an!
Where foot to foot, shoulder to shoulder,
  We climb like the sons of a clan.
There once was a time—and we know it—
  We turned from the Bar with a groan,
Snubbed, gagged, almost jeered at, but, blow it!
  On heather our souls are our own!

In years that are gone, we remember
   Our qualms and dwalms, spasms and fears,
When, briefless from May to September,
   We wound up the Session with tears;
Now papers in boxes go banging,
   And gowns are all whisked out of sight,
When rowans of crimson are hanging,
   And heather with purple is bright!

There once was a man who went fishing
   With Processes under his arm,
And all the long day he was wishing
   His clients might come to no harm;
But jumping and casting at random
   Afforded such excellent play,
That off to their long *avizandum*
   His papers went bobbing away!

The healthiest, hardiest cases
   Are vastly improved with a rest;
Hens, even in snuggest of places,
   Don't always abide on the nest;
The eggs may be yolkless or addled—
   No henwife can prophesy more;
And boats that are leisurely paddled,
   Come ever the best to the shore.

AFRICAN TRADING.

On Afric's shore our Union-Jack
　　Is civilisation's Charter,
And there we teach the simple black
　　The elements of barter :
For ivory tusks, a case of gin ;
　　For palm-oil, kegs of brandy ;
A splash of rum for nuts and gum,
　　Or anything that's handy.

And soon the dusky chief who thinks
　　That fruit-juice made him frisky,
Discovers that all native drinks
　　Are buttermilk to whisky.
And then we sell him spades as good
　　As any pot or kettle,
And knives, whose stomachs turn at wood,
　　As some superior metal.

We teach him also how to run
   In Rule Britannia's traces,
With ball and powder, shot and gun,
   And death at ninety paces.
And, having thus enlarged his views,
   We clothe his smiling fellows
With old red waistcoats, green surtouts,
   And whalebone-ribbed umbrellas.

And yet, this little tale to some
   May seem a string of libels;
For, where we pioneer with rum,
   We follow up with Bibles;
While organs of the Church and Press,
   And bells in every steeple,
Cling, clang, and blow, that righteousness
   Exalts the British people.

A BONNIE WEE WIFIE, O!

YE stirks wha ne'er hae been in love,
    And think them fools an' asses, O!
That praise as blessings from above
    The bonnie winsome lassies, O!
Though ye may hae a cantie lot,
    And cash be rowth an' rifie, O!
You're not a man till ye hae got
    A bonnie wee wifie, O!

        Nae wifie, O! nae wifie, O!
            It's wae and weary single, man!
        But a wifie, O! a wifie, O!
            Gars a' the heart-strings tingle, man!

Just think upon your sisters dear,
    And think on monie others, O!
Wha look sae kindly and sae clear
    On ither sisters' brothers, O!

Think o' the ane whose een sae black,
  Cut through ye like a knifie, O !
And tell me gin she wadna mak'
  A bonnie wee wifie, O !

Indeed, it is a strange affair
  That in life's helter-skelter, O !
Puir folk man toil sae lang and sair
  For food and claes and shelter, O !
And yet the feck o' men will say
  'Tis music like a fifie, O !
To rake and shool and spend it wi'
  A bonnie wee wifie, O !

Though gentle gales fill a' your sails,
  Some nicht it may be blawy, O !
And though your thack be now o' black,
  Some day it will be snawy, O !
When eld comes naggin' at your prime,
  Disturbing a' your lifie, O !
You'll wish that ye had ta'en in time
  A bonnie wee wifie, O !

HAMID THE MAD.

When Nero of Rome was the Ruler,
    He thought it good sport
To crucify Christians on crosses,
    And things of that sort;
Tie women to stakes in the circus,
    And bait them with dogs;
Sew children in skins of wild creatures,
    And spear them like hogs;
With men steeped in tar for his torches
    To light up the ring,
Till Rome stood aghast at the madness
    Of Nero the King.

And now in the East, flaming crimson,
    Sits Hamid the hound,
His tongue dripping lies, and his fingers
    Red blood on the ground;

Rejoicing when heads are rolled earthward,
   And hands are chopped off;
When women are outraged, and children
   Are stabbed with a scoff;
Well pleased when he hears of a village
   In slaughter-pit crammed—
For life is all bloodshed and pillage
   To " Hamid the damned."

Two thousand years gone, and the Romans,
   Alert and alone,
Cried, " Nero is mad ! " and ejected
   The fiend from his throne ;
Two thousand years later, and Europe
   Sustains and permits
A Hamid to stamp out a nation,
   With fire in his wits,
Fiend-haunted, delighting in carnage,
   Transported with blood—
As mad as a wolf that snaps shadows,
   A dog that eats mud !

All green-eyed, all jealous, all silent,
   Bloodguilty as he,
With horse, foot, and cannon encircling,
   And ships on the sea,

F

Round men, women, children, all weeping,
    Unarmed and unscreened,
The nations called Christian are keeping
    A ring for the fiend.
Oh ! would that an angel of heaven
    Would touch from on high
The hearts of the kings, and in pity
    Bid jealousy die !

GOLD-CALF.

Since first for gold-calf on a pole
  A people left its Paschals,
The Law has never had the sole
  Monopoly of rascals.
The car of Juggernaut, we're told,
  Ground down its victims many;
And still the car of shining gold
  Grinds down the dusky penny.

How many wretches and their rags
  Have trickled through the fillers
That yawn above the money-bags
  Of brewers and distillers?
The gold that gilds the gin-saloon
  Was gathered up in coppers:
The sweater's dole, the beggar's boon,
  The bite and sup of paupers.

How many bankrupt traders lie
　　Beneath the broad foundations
On which monopolists now ply
　　Their mighty occupations ?
The diamond star upon his breast
　　Marks but the sole survival
Of all the little lives outprest
　　From every trading rival.

Put not temptation in the way
　　Of weak and witless brothers—
As you'd have others do and say,
　　That say and do to others.
We learnt these things when boys at school,
　　And beardless were our faces ;
And still that very ancient rule
　　Meets many modern cases.

WHEN MAY BECLOUDS THE THORN.

WHEN May beclouds the thorn with fragrant snow,
And unstained cowslips in the pinewoods grow,
When wren and chaffinch leave the window-ledge,
To flirt and twitter in the scant green hedge,
I sought a garden, curiously outlaid
With flowers, and opal gravel, and green blade.
With hand in breast, from walk to walk I wandered ;
With chin in hand, I stood, and looked, and pondered,—
Marking the beds of roses, scarce in leaf,
The yellow daffodils, the tulips brief,
Stunt pansies, with their deeply-dinted shields,
And thought of tilting buttercups in fields ;
Then to the grass I turned my easy tread,
And there beheld the robe of May outspread,
Wove with the firstling daisies still unshorn,
Embroidered with crocus' bright lanthorn.
And then methought—May is the time of grasses,
Which not a month in Summer's prime surpasses.

The blackbird hailed me from the orchard wall,
And then I sought the fruit-trees rising tall,
Beneath their wood to look a rigging through
Of rosy blossoms laid against the blue ;
Like Aaron-rods, with upward pointing clear,
They held aloft the promise of the year.
Already to mine eye, above my head
In clusters hung the cherry, burning red ;
Embowered in leaves, the ruddy apple swung ;
The purple plum from bending branches hung ;
And like a plummet fathoming the air
Did dip and rise the tapered russet pear.
And then methought—More sweet than grassy bosom
Are May's white arms that sift the air with blossom.

This is my orchard, where the winds make laughter,
That jollity and fruit may follow after ;
The flowers of promise in these pages find,
And fruit will gather in a merry mind :
For he who knows not when to bend and laugh
Has scarcely learnt philosophy by half ;
But he who mingles humour with his life,
Has found a cushion in a world of strife.

THE MINISTER'S ANN.

You've often heard tell o' the Kirk on the Green,
  The manse and the minister's man,
But, out or in parish, I trow you've ne'er seen
  The jaud ca'd the Minister's Ann!

A lawyer makes love to a guid-ganging plea,
  A dog to a het parritch-pan;
A blackbird has een for a ripe cherry-tree,
  A Minister een for his Ann.

No castle can keep her o' mortar and stane,
  Or kirkyard, frae Sheba to Dan;
She's aye at her best when the Minister's gane,
  Sae vaunty and jaunty is Ann!

And then the strange beckings and booings begin—
  Explain and expound them who can;
His widow and bairns—or for that, next o' kin—
  Are muckle ta'en up wi' their Ann!

For Ann, let me say, is no ghaist in a bleeze,
  Or gowk wi' a feather and fan,
But half a year's teinds, when the Minister dees,
  And that's the bit thing they ca' Ann !

And aft the incomer looks dour as a Turk,
  To find all their spunes in his pan ;
But, lick it or leave it, six months he man work
  To pay the bit tocher o' Ann !

DANCING DAFFODILS.

WHEN the brown thrush, on slender spray,
With rousing note brings in the day ;
When twinkling of the snowdrop bell
Is heard by shepherds in the dell,—
Let surly Winter bang the door,
Though loud his bark, his bite is o'er.

When dancing daffodils unfold
Their lemon caps and frills of gold ;
When coltsfoot and the daisy pass
With starry steps upon the grass,—
Be meadows green or meadows white,
Gruff Winter's rod is broken quite.

And now, wherever Hebe goes,
Pale woodbine and the red wild rose
Their honeyed petals strain apart
To catch her image on their heart,
And say, no flower in their retreat
Is half so modest, half so sweet !

THE SCOTTIFICATION OF ENGLAND.*

HEIGH-HO! for the bat and the ball,
  The bales, the leggings, the wicket—
Short cut was the favourite of all
  Who last were fielders at cricket.
The kings of the willow have run
  To ash, for fresh inspiration ;
The triumph of golf has begun
  With England's Scottification !

Adieu to the net and the court,
  The ball, the racket of tennis !
Deuce all, and One love, are, in short,
  As rare as hansoms in Venice.
The maidens and youths of degrees
  Have fled, in glad perturbation,
To help on with hazards and tees
  All England's Scottification !

* Mr A. J. Balfour's speech at Chiselhurst, 1894.

Farewell to the lawn and the hoop,
 The pin, the mallet of croquet,
Where rovers were pegged with a whoop!
 And roll and rattle of roquet :
What once to the curate was bliss
 Is now a tame occupation,
Compared with a putt and a miss
 For England's Scottification !

Instead of the racket and bat,
 Are cleek, and iron, and brassy ;
Half-volley, and Vantage, and that,
 Are Topped, and Stimied, and Grassy ;
A ball and a stick, if you please,
 Have wrought this grand transformation,
With foursomes, and twosomes, and threes,
 In England's Scottification !

When bagpipes are heard in the land,
 With drone and chanter and whistle,
All golfers will quite understand
 The Rose has knelt to the Thistle ;
When Cockneys wear kilts and take snuff,
 And Putt with due moderation,
The proof will be ample enough
 Of England's Scottification !

RIDE A MILE.

Ride a mile on daddy's foot!
  Up and ride away,
Round about the misty hill,
  In among the hay.
Out upon the whinny moor,
  Doun the windy glen;
Out and in among the trees,
  Through the wood again.

Now we climb a grassy bank
  Where the violets grow;
Now we canter down again
  To the road below.
Now we pass the miller's door,
  See him as he stands!
With the meal so floury white
  On his face and hands.

When the moon is round and white,
  Fairies play their tricks,
Riding races through the sky
  All on crooked sticks:
Who that has so fleet a horse
  Would not up and ride
Round the world on daddy's foot,
  By the chimneyside?

Bonnie bairn, with cheeks so red,
  You have ridden well—
Some day you will have to go
  Through the world yoursel';
Then you'll be a mighty man,
  Tramping on your feet,—
May you keep a heart as kind,
  And a laugh as sweet.

COCKIELEERIE-LAW.*

Six legal wigs, like well-plumed tappit hens,
Sat brooding o'er a pair of fighting cocks;
While lesser wigs, begowned, and brief in hand,
Declaimed in flowing periods of the fray,
Like ancient bards, that wanted but their harps,
Their wallets, ballad verse, and song, to make
The very goose-quills, sleeping on the bench,
Awake! take sides, and spill each other's ink.
And as they spake, a legal fog dropt down
Upon the learned six, and each beheld,
In green mirage, born of the cloud of words,
Two cocks, Game-cocks, crop-combed, erect, and slim,
With feathers dipped in crimson, blue, and gold,
Frill-necked, with trailing wings, and spurs of steel,

* In full Court, Edinburgh, 23rd December 1892.

That on each other flew and pecked and spurred,
Spurred, pecked, and flew again, until the Court
Reeled like a cock-pit, and the crowd of wigs—
Of boyish idle wigs—took bonnet shapes
That hooded scowling brows of cursing men,
Who laid their bets on this bird and on that,
As, with quick panting breath and beaks agape,
They pranced, flew, fought, until the oaken bar
Was spattered o'er with feathers and cock-blood.
At length one cock the other overthrew,
And struck quick spurs into his quivering breast
Until he died; then he, with croaking crow,
Fell, wounded, bleeding, dying by his side,
Amid the applauding cheers of thirsty throats,
Soon to be slaked with liquid bets—and so
The battle ended, but the fog remained.

A rustling of silk plumes upon the bench,
Five wigs bent low, and thus great Solon spake :—

" 'Twas in Kilbarchan that this fight was fought,
And straight the men who prompted it were ta'en,
And jailed, and tried, and sentenced for the same ;
But now they seek release, and this their plea,
That in the gracious Act which says that men
Shall not treat brutes and beasts with cruelty,

The name of " *Cock* " is absent; therefore they
Claim full exemption for their brutish deeds,
And we, vicegerents of our gentle Queen,
With spectacle on nose, must well explore
This vital point in *Cockieleerie-law.*

" The illumined page of history reveals
Cock-fighting as an ancient royal sport.
The Greeks and later Romans in their day
Found pastime sweet in setting cock on cock ;
Profound Themistocles took keen delight
In battling fowls; the glorious Cæsar, too,
Loved much to back his bird ; and, furthermore,
Mark Antony's game-cocks did always lose
When pitted against Cæsar's fiercer breed.
King Henry VIII., of sainted memory !
At Whitehall had a special cock-pit built,
Wherein his royal birds made lively sport
For gentle dames and all his merry knights.
The most accomplished scholar of his day,
Squire Roger Ascham, tutor to Queen Bess,
Much as he loved his books, loved cocks the more,
And loved them most when victors in the fight.
And last of all, that great and noble duke,
The conqueror of Blenheim, in game-birds
Found something that reminded him of self;

And thus we see the fighting instinct strong
In cocks, and other nobles of past time.

" Game-cocks, we find, from earliest Cockereldom,
Delight in war, as dogs to bark and bite,
And raining blows upon each other's ribs
Do best fulfil their part of nature's plan,
Which built them slim and bade them love the fray;
And while we hope no preference here to show,
'Tis open question whether rearing fowls
To wring their necks, or match them in the pit,
Does more exalt the brute or sink the man.

" But here, the cocks were armed with spurs of steel,
And 'tis a subtle question, whether they
With iron shod, or spurred with native horn,
Do deal the deadliest blows in angry fray;
And, while we have our own opinion strong !
'Tis not within our province to pronounce.

" If it be wrong with steel to prick a fowl,
What of the spurs with which hard riders goad
The bleeding sides of horses in the race,
Or panting steeplechase, or country hunt ?
And what of hares in coursing run to death ?
Of quivering foxes torn by yelling hounds ?

Of wheeling pigeons slaughtered for a prize?
We make no mention of the common use
Of otter-hunting, grouse- and pheasant-drives,
And of the sport termed noble! where the stag
Is forced upon the guns that lay him low.
No doubt, two blacks can never make one white,
Nor multiplying blacks turn black to grey;
But if to brutalise the man be thought amiss,
Then there are other ways than fighting cocks.

" Still that's beside our purpose, which is this—
To scan the Statute, microscope in hand,
And note if in its sweep humane we see
A roosting-place for crowing Chanticleer;
And there we find, or rather fail to find,
The name of " Cock " among the saving list
Of nineteen beasts protected by the law,
Though thus the tale concludes, " *and other kinds
Of animals domestic,*" or like words.
Are we to find Game-cocks domestic fowls?
Are we to hold that birds are animals?
Our view is quite the contrary, or else
There's not a beast, bird, fish, or insect but
The term " domestic " would to them apply,
And make it penal e'en to slay a louse.

" And while, in other parts of this same Act,
We find " Cock " followed by the general phrase,
" *Or other kind of animal,*" we hold
It bears not on the matter now in hand,
But only serves to show that Parliament,
When brooding, clucking, hen-like, o'er this Act,
Had Cocks well in her eye, and plainly did,
Of purpose full, omit them from the list ;
And while bear-fights, bull-fights, dog-fights, and all
Vile sports and brutish cruelty to beasts,
The spirit and the letter of the law
Do quite forbid, *Unanimous we hold*
Cock-fighting is a lawful use of cocks,
And finding so, we liberate these men.

" It will be said, this Statute has been read
Conversely in our sister England, where
It is the Charter of proud Chanticleer ;
But what of that ?   It alters not our mind !
But only shows that they, of feebler clay,
Stick not at trifles, so the end be good,
And let the heart o'erbeat the legal mind ;
While we, of sterner stuff, fail not to find
Motes in the sunshine of their simple wits,
And gnats to strain out of their cups of wine ;

For, in the nice accomplishment and use
Of splitting hairs and weighing feathers small,
Of riddling wisdom from a peck of words,
We are more skilled, more subtle, more profound
Than are our legal brethren of the South."

Whereat five horse-hair wigs again bowed down
In low obeisance to the greater sage,
And straight the Court was cleared of Cocks and men.

A LONG, LONG DRIVE.

BRING me my golf-clubs, lay them down,
   And tee the ball, my laddie !
For I'm a golfer from the town,
   And you shall be my caddie.

     For there's nought so sweet,
     When the day is fine,
     As a long, long drive
     In a straight, straight line !

And now, if I should miss my stroke,
   And seem a bit bamboozled,
I trust you'll say, by way of joke,
   Tee-shots are ofttimes foozled !

In my approach, if with my cleek
   I send the soft turf flying,
I hope you'll mention, if you speak,
   Hard strokes are aye worth trying.

And if upon the putting-green
  I lift when I should roll it,
Be sure you tell me you have seen
  Good putts oft fail to hole it.

With these few precepts kept in view,
  Let's open out our battery,
For I've observed, and so have you,
  Small coins change hands with flattery.

WINSOME JENNY.

Winsome Jenny 'mang the hay—
 Raking, shaking, raking, shaking—
Stole young Jockey's heart away,—
 Dear the laddie lo'ed her.
  Was it pleasure, was it pride?
  Still she held her head aside,
  Saying, she could ne'er abide
 False young men that wooed her.

Jockey is a blithesome boy!
 Laughing, daffing, laughing, daffing;
All his skill he did employ
 Jenny's heart to ravage.
  First he spoke her fair and well,
  Next he praised her sister Nell,
  Then he left her to hersel'—
 Heartless, cruel savage!

Growing love is like a pirn—
    Winding, binding, winding, binding ;
Jockey kissed her at the kirn,
    When he came to meet her.
        " Lassie ! lay thy hand in mine ! "
        " Laddie ! I am thine ! thine ! thine ! "
        Faithful love is like good wine—
    Aulder, aye the sweeter.

THE WEE WHITE HOUSE.

THE wee white house among the trees
   Beside the sandy shore,
With roses on the gable-end
   And fuchsias at the door ;
It faded slowly from my sight
   Across the gurly sea,
But ah ! it is the dearest place
   In all the world for me !

By day I ken the gowden sun
   Beams on my bairnies twa,
And whiles they warstle on the green,
   And whiles they kick the ba'.
By night I think yon wandering moon
   That looms alang the deep,
Keeks in on Minnie mending claes
   For twa wee rogues asleep.

The Duke has got his castles three,
    Each with a different name,
And silken beds and roofs of gold,
    But where has he his hame ?
The lark that skims the wide blue air,
    Back to his nest man flee—
And fondly aye my thoughts return
    Hame, wife and weans, to thee !

THE KING'S HIE-WAY.*

ARGUMENT.

ANE man, be the king's hie-way,
  Is ca'in' ane tup and ane wedder,
And sae that they gang na astray,
  Wi' tow they are taigled togedder.
Be-chance, ane puir horse in their track
  Upon the said hie-way is sleepand,
Streeked oot at his ease, wi' sair back,
  And nane sort of guard the while keepand.

Ane scheip to the richt gangs apart,
  And ane to the left gies a gallup—
The tow gies the sair back a scart,
  And waukens the horse wi' a wallup:

* A reported case in the time of King David II.

Quherethrow the said horse, richt or wrang,
  Is moved to rise up, wi' tail swingand,
And aff at a trot he bode gang,
  Wi' scheips on ilk side o' him hingand.

Swith, hither and thither he rins,
  Throw neip-fields and sundrie like places,
Until to a miln yett he wins,
  The end o' his cantrips and paces:
In time, he loups throw the miln dure,
  The tow on his back scarting deeper,
Where peats are in lowe on the flure,—
  A miln and a fire without keeper!

The peats being scattered, the miln
  Is brent, and all in it togedder
Are reestit as white as ane kiln,
  Horse, halter, corn, tup, tow, and wedder :—
Demanded, a verdict on aith,
  Quhilk stands the ill-dune, and ill-doer?
And quha sall mak' guid a' this skeath?
  And quhilk's the pursued and pursuer?

VERDICT.

Replied—The said horse sall first pay
  For scheips that were brent intill mutton—

For why, on the king's free hie-way
   Is not where he sauld hae doun-sutton :
The miller sall pay for the horse,
   And scheips, that so hetly were ended—
For why, he left open, of course,
   His dure, with ane fire unattended.

Likewise, be it furder declared,
   For guid of the king and his lieges,
Said road sall be forthwith repaired
   To fourteen feet brede, 'tween the hedges ;
That he quha hath cause to ca' scheip,
   May ca' them in safety and leizure,
And he quha's sick horse fa's asleep,
   May let the puir beast hae his pleezure.

FREE EDUCATION.

A FANCY took the nation
   In the year of '72,
That spreading education
   Was the proper thing to do ;
And with much trumpet-blowing
   There was passed the golden rule—
In sunning or in snowing,
   Every child must go to school.

The law that was so pressing
   Had an unforeseen result,
It brought the poor their blessing
   Like a stone and catapult ;
For when the hard-pressed father
   Came to pay the School Board fees,
With sudden blow it rather
   Brought the father to his knees.

When children's claims were sorest,
　　With a row of mouths to fill,
Then hardest on the poorest
　　Fell this splendid golden bill;
Howe'er he might be willing,
　　It is more than man can do
To make one silver shilling
　　Do the splendid work of two.

And so the wives went trudging
　　Where the husbands would not trudge,
And heard the Sheriff judging
　　What he little cared to judge;
Who told them, from their coppers
　　They must pay the School Board fees,
Or seek relief, like paupers,
　　On their very humble knees.

Now, when the nation tells us
　　We must learn our A B C,
As far as it compels us,
　　Education should be free;
Which means that by taxation,
　　Weighing purses here and there,
The rich should pay their ration,
　　And the poor should pay their share.

We like to hear on Sunday
    That the strong should help the weak ;
And if upon the Monday
    We would practise what we speak—
Then nothing can be surer
    Than that each his purse should draw,
And richer help the poorer,
    Be the spirit of the law.

SWEARING.

SOME swear by the water of Ganges,
   And some with their hats on their head,
And some kiss the cross on the Bible,
   And some kiss the Koran instead—
While some on a plate
Swear oaths that are great,
   And break them like bread.

And all, whether heathen or Christian,
   Mohammedan, Hindu, or Norse,
Declare that the absence of swearing
   Robs language of half of its force—
And soldiers and sailors,
And tinkers and tailors,
   Cry ditto, of course !

King William, to stop profanation,
　　Most wisely enacted an Act
Abolishing oaths that are idle,
　　And saying with tartness and tact,
That plain declarations
And short affirmations
　　Are better, in fact.

And subsequent Acts have repeated
　　That men are quite right everywhere
To kick against oaths when examined,
　　And free to affirm and declare ;
But, somehow or other,
The world and his brother
　　Continue to swear.

An eagle objecting to freedom,
　　A skylark preferring a cage,
Are not half so foolish and feeble
　　As men with the brow of a sage,
Who, with choice of both,
Prefer the great oath
　　In this Christian age.

The broom is all broidered with brightness
　　With catching the sun's golden ball,

The hawthorn is mantled in whiteness
 With drinking the dews as they fall,—
Swear not, we are told,
By the Temple, or gold,
 But, swear not at all !

RING, BELLS OF BLUE.

OH, were my love a shepherd lass
  Her cows from pasture bringing,
I'd meet her in the clover-grass
  Where sweet bluebells are ringing ;
I'd tell her that each drop of dew
  For me its heart was breaking,
And all the little bells of blue
  At her their heads were shaking.

And should she say, they need not grieve,
  Nor bow their heads in pity,
I'd pluck my courage by the sleeve,
  And pipe a livelier ditty ;
I'd tell her that each drop that fell
  A tear of joy was shedding,
And every little dancing bell
  Was ringing for a wedding.

Blow, blow, ye gentle winds, and tie
   Love-knots among her tresses,
And say, my lips are parched and dry
   For lack of her caresses;
Ring, bells of blue on slender spray,
   And bid farewell to sorrow,
For if she pities me to-day,
   She'll marry me to-morrow.

THE CROFTER'S PLEA.

A BIT of land beside the loch,—
  His Lordship's sacred water,—
Damp walls, a leaky roof, but hoch !
  He's just a Highland cottar !
From rising sun to closing day
  He's at it late and early,
With rake and fork among the hay,
  And scythe among the barley.

Each time he paid his annual rent,
  It seemed a bit one-sided
That the small blessings nature sent
  Should be so ill divided :
A bite to him who owned the soil,
  A crumb to him who tilled it,
And bigger bites for leave to toil,
  Whene'er the factor willed it.

One day the Roving Judges came
   And looked in at his village,
And saw the stones that went by name
   Of pasturage and tillage;
'Twas then the factor's face grew red,
   The cottar's well contented,
When his small place, they plainly said,
   For years had been rack-rented.

When poor men rob the rich, I'm sure,
   It's bad enough and blameful;
But when the rich men rob the poor,
   It's fifty times more shameful.
Rogues clad in velvet ride their nags
   Along our public highways,
While honest men, in earth-soiled rags,
   Toil in our fields and byways.

Since Courts can cancel all the sludge
   Of long years of oppression,
When all's paid up, perhaps some Judge,
   In his most wise discretion,
Will put a landlord on the rack
   To better his repenting,
And bid him pay the cottar back
   The fruits of his rack-renting.

FAREWELL TO THE COT.

Farewell to the cot 'mong the whins and the bracken,
  The sand in the bay, and the rocks on the shore,
To deep-sounding Staffa, and beauteous Kyleakin—
  I leave thee, perhaps to return never more.
The birds sing as sweet by thy clear springing fountains,
  The sun shines as bright on the hills and the sea,
But o'er thy deep valleys and high swelling mountains
  The soft winds of freedom no longer blow free.

Green straths to the sheep have been given without
    measure,
  And glens to the deer, for the stranger to kill,
And all for a proud chieftain's profit or pleasure,
  Thy clans are dispersed like the mist on the hill.
Where once were the hamlets, the shielings, the gardens,
  And rustic contentment and industry dwelt,
Cold hearths, ruined walls, and green mounds are the
    wardens
  That mark the last home of the poor banished Celt.

But who can forget, as he treads the red heather,
  And hears the lost voices that rise on the breeze,
The men who have gone in their hundreds together
  To crowd the dark cities, or cross the wide seas?
I'd rather for life be a poor humble toiler,
  With conscience from shame and from cruelty clear,
Than of lonely hearths be a careless despoiler,
  To make them the home of the sheep and the deer.

The nation that sleeps while her children are banished,
  That stood like a guard round her wave-beaten shore,
Will some day awake with a cry to the vanished,
  A cry for the feet that return never more.
My breast heaves with sighs as I leave thee for ever,
  To think that man's pleasure should work such deep
    woe;—
Forget thy dear mountains? Ah! no, I shall never,
  Forget thee till Highland blood ceases to flow.

THE SHERIFF'S FAREWELL.*

Gone are the days of plea and proof,
  Of parties, prayers, and pleadings,
Of precedents, of warp and woof,
  And dark conundrum readings ;
Gone are the days upon the Bench
  Of weariness and waiting,
Beneath the dreary drip and drench
  Of speeches and debating.

No more to sit till nature fails,
  And back and limbs are aching,
Holding aloft the golden scales
  That to and fro are shaking ;
No more to toil with cramping pen
  O'er sheets of foolscap paper,
Recording thoughts of many men—
  Some water, and some vapour.

* Sheriff Erskine Murray, Glasgow, 1897.

Farewell the bench! farewell the Bar!
    For six-and-thirty sessions
I've known what work and duty are,
    And striv'n to learn their lessons.
Now Nature warns me I must rest,
    And I obey the call;
I've only tried to do my best—
    Good-bye! God bless you all!

No kinder heart e'er wore a gown
    Or pondered a decision,
No gentler hand put evil down,
    Or sent a rogue to prison.
Like him, may we rejoice to know,
    As life runs to its end,
That we have never made a foe,
    And never lost a friend.

WHAT IS YOUR LIFE.

WHAT is your life?   A wayside flower
That spreads, and blooms its little hour
In cloud and sunshine, wind and rain,
Then droops to earth its head again.

A vapour and a cloud of white
That swims in fields of azure light,
Wind-blown, sun-kiss'd, till close of day,
When sombre-hued, it fades away.

The gift of God !   A heavenly birth,
Seen through the vestures of this earth—
A star that whitens e'er the dawn,
By Him who loves, and gave, withdrawn.

Oh help me so to count my days
That I may walk in wisdom's ways,
And feel when light and life grow dim
The hand that leads me back to Him.

SWEET PRIMROSE LOCKS.

TRICKED with a tress of yellow hair,
  Tied in a knot of ribbon blue,
With ruddy lips, a pouting pair,
  And dimpled cheeks of rosy hue ;
I run to fetch her little glove,
  I kneel to tie her muddy shoe—
Oh ! what a case, to be in love
  With Primrose Locks, of two times two !

She speaks of rains that wash the sky,
  Of Mr Wind and Mrs Snow,
And when she hymns her " Home on High ! "
  She sings about her " Hime on Ho ! "
Who hangs the leaves upon the tree ?
  Who paints the rose, and makes it grow ?
Who broke the moon ? and who made me ?
  Are things she much would like to know.

She builds foundations sure and broad
   Of cubes and squares that meet and mix ;
She frowns when things go kind of odd,
   And what she does not like she kicks.
One day she asked me who made God :
   The answer found her at her tricks,
For with a little frown and nod
   She brought to earth her tower of bricks.

Sweet Primrose Locks, you've oft been told
   The stars are not all silver dust,
The sun is not a plate of gold,
   And wallflowers are not stained with rust.
You doubt such stories, I suppose,
   Believing only when you must ;
But there are things which no one knows,
   And what we do not know we trust.

THE FAIRY-FOLK.

COME cuddle close in daddy's coat
   Beside the fire so bright,
And hear about the fairy-folk
   That wander in the night;
For when the stars are shining clear
   And all the world is still,
They float across the hollow moon
   From hill to cloudy hill.

Their caps are red, their cloaks are green,
   Their tassels, silver bells,
And when they shake them in the wind
   The merry ringing swells.
With stirrups on the crimson moth,
   And saddles on his wings,
They gallop down the purple sky
   With golden bridle-rings.

They come to visit girls and boys,
  And see how sound they sleep,
To stand beside their cosy cots
  And in their faces peep ;
For in the whole of fairy-land
  They know no sweeter sight
Than little children sleeping sound,
  With faces rosy bright.

On tiptoe crowding round their heads,
  When bright the moonlight beams,
They chirp and whisper little words
  That fill the mind with dreams ;
And when they see a sunny smile,
  With rosy finger-tips
They lay a hundred kisses sweet
  Upon the ruddy lips.

Then all the crimson-spotted moths
  Spread out their shining wings,
And bear away the fairy crowd
  With shaking bridle-rings.
Come cuddle close in daddy's coat
  Beside the fire so bright—
Perhaps the little fairy-folk
  Will visit you to-night.

ADVICE TO A YOUNG LAWYER.

Into the ink-pot o' the Law
You've ta'en the jump, and doo or daw,
There ye maun sprachle, kick, and claw
        Amang queer cattle;
And syne, my rhyming horn I'll blaw,
        And spring my rattle.

At College ye hae learnt the grace
O' steady work, wi' dour-set face;
For he that wad keep up the pace
        Man hae ticht sails—
Sheer industry aft wins the race
        Where genius fails.

Wigs cockin' on a bench, you'll find,
Much like the lave o' human kind—

This way disposed, that way inclined,
  Wi' nip and nudge,—
A modest story, bear in mind,
  Cleeks aye the judge.

However changed be mood or tense,
Plain common law is common-sense ;
The Court may ring wi' pounds and pence,
  But ne'er forget,
The core o' a' the foil and fence
  Is Justice yet !

Lend not your tongue to the abuse
Of sober truth, let no dog-noose
Your conscience thraw or heart seduce
  Wi' glints o' gold,—
Success is but a poor excuse
  For honour sold.

Langsyne the wee bit writer body
Was pented black's a tinker's cuddy—
A fause-tongued loon, sly, inky duddy,
  Snuffy and drucken ;
But now, frae these he stands stark scuddy,
  And clean oot shucken.

Behold him now wi' glozened knees
Wafflin' a scrimpit table o' fees
Ower twa three sticks frae twa three trees,
   Aft green and wat,
Greetin' through reek to mak' a bleeze
   And boil his pat !

Some men grow rich wi' tricks and plots,
And some wi' scrapings-oot and blots,
But there are guineas poor as groats
   To him that won them :
May your half-crowns hae nae black spots
   O' brunstane on them !

Shun michty hills and lownsome ditches,
For little threeds mak' siccar stitches,
And neither poverty nor riches
   Will be your lot—
Among the Law's queer kinks and hitches
   An honest Scot !

And whiles you'll gie a helping hand
To poor folk in a weary land,—
What though your fee be sma' as sand
   Upon the dredger,
Sic kindly acts will rank and stand
   Right side the ledger !

And now, farewell! this Scriever's screed
Some day may stand you in guid steed—
To keep your heart up, were indeed
      Weel worth a letter :
Where I hae failed, may you succeed,
      And e'en do better !

NO MORE A-GOLFING.

His face was shapen like the sphinx—
  Mark well what I am saying—
I met him golfing on the links,
  As childlike as yon babe of Ginx.

    I'll go no more a-golfing
      With you, my boy !

You've heard how simple fish are gaffed ?—
  Mark well what I am saying—
Although he never joked or laughed,
  Each hole of mine he always halved.

While I was gazing all around—
  Mark well what I am saying—
His little ball he always found
  At rest upon a rising ground.

I softly kept his little score—
    Mark well what I am saying—
And then he taught me of his lore,
    That three and two are sometimes *four*.

I played the round out with my sphinx—
    Mark well what I am saying—
With outward smiles and inward winks,—
    On that or any other links,

      I'll go no more a-golfing
      With you, my boy!

THE HILL WAS ROBED WITH HEATHER.

THE hill was robed with heather, and the wind
Did offer honey'd incense to my mind;
Surrounding slopes were cloven white with streams
That dropt in silence, and like voiceless dreams,
Whene'er a grey cloud rolled athwart the sun,
Swift feet of shadows round my hill did run,
And passed out on the sea, whose silver furrow
Was quenched as with a hush of passing sorrow.
Heigh-ho! the vast does ever work this folly
Of turning little minds to melancholy.
But soon, behind the mountain's purple shoulder,
A bright thought came, that winged my fancy bolder—
A red sail, small, but joyously upreared,
Above a varnished, shining boat appeared;
Another, and another, shot in view,
Swift bending o'er the waves of windy blue.

"Hurrah!" I said, "stout hearts are stiff to beat;
It is the outward-going fishing fleet."
And as the glad wind tipped their gunwales o'er,
I marked their brown nets heaped in ample store.

Methinks I've dropped my net and trailed my hook,
And all my fishing's in this little book :
From year to year, with mingled skill and erring,
I've hooked my mackerel, taken in my herring,
To bring to all, as each true fisher should,
The freshest fare for body and brain food;
And now, go laugh? when wit and truth unite,
There's phosphorus and fun in that small bite.

PRINTED BY WILLIAM BLACKWOOD AND SONS.

www.ingramcontent.com/pod-product-compliance
Lightning Source LLC
Chambersburg PA
CBHW031121020726
47495CB00007B/2300